Exiles and Marriages

Exiles
and
Marriages

by

Donald Hall

New York

The Viking Press

1956

PUBLISHED BY THE VIKING PRESS IN NOVEMBER 1955

PUBLISHED ON THE SAME DAY IN THE DOMINION OF CANADA
BY THE MACMILLAN COMPANY OF CANADA LIMITED

SECOND PRINTING MARCH 1956

Acknowledgment is made to the following magazines in which some of the poems in this book
originally appeared: *The Atlantic, Audience, Har-
per's Magazine, Harvard Advocate, Hudson Review, Ladies' Home Journal, Mademoiselle, New
Orleans Poetry Journal, New Republic, New Ven-
tures, The New Yorker, Paris Review, Pegasus
Publications, Poetry,* and *Western Review;* and also
to *New World Writing 5.*

Library of Congress catalog card number: 56-5073

PRINTED IN U. S. A. BY THE VAIL-BALLOU PRESS, INC.

For Donald A. Hall, Sr., and Lucy Wells Hall,

in love and gratitude

Contents

5. THE STRANGERS

6. EXILES

7. MARRIAGES

1. Conduct and Work

WEDDING PARTY

The pock-marked player of the accordion
Empties and fills his squeeze box in the corner,
Kin to the tiny man who pours champagne,
Kin to the caterer. These solemn men,
Amid the sounds of silk and popping corks,
Stand like pillars. And the white bride
Moves through the crowd as a chaired relic moves.

We are the guest invited yesterday,
Friend to the bride's rejected suitor, come
On sudden visit unexpectedly.
And so we chat, on best behavior, with
The Uncle, Aunt, and unattractive girl;
And watch the summer twilight melt away
As thunder gathers head to end the day.

And all at once the pock-marked player grows
To overwhelming greatness by the bride,
Whose marriage withers to a rind of years,
Old photographs behind the attic door;
And in the storm that hurls upon the room
Above the crowd he holds his breathing box
That only empties, fills, empties, fills.

3

Anarchic badlands spread without a road,
And from the river west no turned-up loam;
No farmer prayed for rain, no settler's horse
But one time blundered riderless to home.

Unfriendly birds would gather in the air,
A circling kind of tombstone. As for the law,
No marshal lived for long unless he could
Defeat his mirror'd image to the draw.

So now he rode upon a silver horse.
He stood for law and order. Anarchy
Like flood or fire roared through every gate
But he and Tonto hid behind a tree,

And when the bandits met to split the loot,
He blocked the door. With silver guns he shot
The quick six-shooters from their snatching hands,
And took them off to jail and let them rot.

For him the badlands were his mother's face.
He made an order where all order lacked,
From Hanged Boy Junction to the Rio Grande.
Why did he wear a mask? He was abstract.

A FRIEND REVISITED

Beside the door
She stood whom I had known before.
I saw the work of seven years
In graying hair and worried eyes,
And in a smile:
"Find in me only what appears,
And let me rest a while."

Though it had not been honesty
Always to say the sudden word
When she was young,
I liked the old disguise
Better than what I heard—
False laughter on the tongue
That once had made all efforts to seem free.

I do not ask for final honesty,
Since none can say,
"This is my motive, this is me,"
But I will pray
Deliberation and a shaping choice
To make a speaking voice.

Now bleak December seeds the London street
And on these twisted weeds all weathers beat.

One makes for silver out of painful chalk
Vague Helens where the solid shopclerks walk.

Another limbless sits with groping eye
To grapple pity from the passer-by.

I drop a sixpence in the luckless box
To bribe the devil and avoid the pox,

But must assume the spidery cripple's crutch
Because my fingers use their silver touch.

A NOVELIST

Although a Protestant of Niebuhr's crew,
   And fond of evil in a work of art,
On most occasions she was sure she knew
   That goodness was the scheme of every heart.

In her democracy of honest men,
   There was no need for hell, and she ignored it.
Depressive cycles came and came again
   Out of this tension: she had not explored it.

For when some upstart critic criticized
   Her novels much too harshly for their worth,
She saw beneath the critic's prose, disguised,
   The wretched horns of Satan poking forth.

But still her characters were good and strong,
   With social evils as the only ill.
Her small success did not endure for long—
   Even the public finally had its fill.

Her first response was innocent surprise
   That everyone could fail to understand;
She stiffened up, she made no compromise,
   But wrote as ever, dull and second-hand.

Still the young men were laughing at her name.
   At last, with nothing left her but despair,
She mounted a tall building and became
   A form of horror on the hellish air.

CONDUCT AND WORK

1

I am no Faust: unsalaried my sin;
It is from love I ask the devil in.

2

From flour of love and sweet of guilt I make
For much long eating, such a cruel cake,

Until Socratic age exchanges it
For bread and water of the naked wit.

3

My days, my years, are vexed
    By death to magnify
My self that must perfect
    Its utterance and die.

4

I turned and turned
    But, left alone,
Looked through my hand
    And saw the bone.

5

Humanity perfectible, and good?
There is a smell of sulphur in that shade;
To hasten goodness we employ the gun
And take thereby inequitable gain,
While at our liberal anxieties
Laughs democratic Mephistopheles.

6

EPITAPH ON AN ARMY

Good men were brave to honor a command,
Who died in anger. Death was never cheap.
Stranger, they kept invaders from the land,
And yet there is no peace that men will keep.

7

The rot that eats the poem up
Comes from the face I learned at school,
When over every friendly cup
I smiled to suffer any fool.

8

What blithe impeccability designed
Plays games upon the fringes of the mind,
But wisdom with a sweet array of facts
Cleaves to the mental center like an ax.

9

Hanging fire can be no use unless
You pot them when they think you're weaponless.

10

How God hath labored to produce the duck!
Some call it skill, but I'd say it was luck.

11

Poetical *Philander* only thought to love:
He went to bed with what the girls were symbols of.

12

I learned in a vision a secret that nobody knows:
Criticism must be at least as well written as prose.

13

O Aphrodite, fine and nothing loath,
Is it the touch, the answering, or both?
When that sweet action is at last unloosed,
How can you tell seducer from seduced?

APOLOGY

1

These mirrors give my face its truest frame.
Look at my pose: I mimic for the crowd
Sequent like couplets to my glittered name—
My horde of eyes that mirrors shout aloud.

My poems posture less, but primp and stand
Like manikins I made in my despite
And hate their maker—not to understand
What fire it was that gave me working light.

That face was made with only mimicry,
No virtue in it and no innocence
To swing the hero's sword, but irony
That lives on words and must reverse their sense.

But now the sun must pose on me all day
And I have come to where those poems end.
I stand alone and weaponless to say
That my small mouth is broken. I must mend.

2

Huge beasts confront me on this mountainside
And I am weak to battle them to death,
But in old books I find a practiced guide;
Heroic song fills out my coward breath.

There is a virtue which I must achieve
Whose struggle will decide this heavy change,
A singleness, whose excellence must leave
This personal mountain for a greater range.

Now irony is weary on my tongue.
I close the wound to yield the subtle bow.
The beasts are real whose shapes I walk among.
I bury the cheap magic that I know.

Now with my single voice I speak to you.
I do not hear an echo to my voice.
I walk the single path that heroes do
And climb the mountain which is my own choice.

White bone in the yellow flats of sun,
bone in the flutes of rain.
The years of stone are twenty-four; this hill of stone,
a skeleton to guard a yard of bone,
thrown by the windy guns of men together,
aspires to no heaven but the hill.

Ictinus built it; Pentelic marble brought
by the wealth of ships;
upraised, the columns breathed
in curves of marble.
Now bones breathe thinly in the yellow sun.
The architectures strive.

Beyond the city now to guard the hill
enormous guns and wealth
from the Baltic Sea to the Red
and through the Pacific to the Asian coast
as Romans stood
four hundred years along the Danube River
to guard both granaries and temples.

They guard your skull
who lie and breathe across from me—
but an empty house of bone.
This architecture too
breathes in the yellow sun
and does not lose;

but keep the Turk away, and the slaughtering Hun,
who prey on such infirmity.

Infirm and wise,
fed by the stone,
to catch the sun.

SYLLABLES OF A SMALL FIG TREE

I am dead, to be sure,
for thwarting Christ's pleasure,
Jesus Christ called Saviour.

I was a small fig tree.
Unjust it seems to me
that I should withered be.

If justice sits with God,
Christ is cruel Herod
and I by magic dead.

If there is no justice
where great Jehovah is,
I will the devil kiss.

The hugy spider stooping through the door
Rushes to kiss me, but I am not there;
I have retreated through the cunning floor
And hear him flounder at the empty air;
I sit in my concealment, smiling
To hear him weep and swear;
And now the keepers come with candy,
He
Will need no more beguiling.

These sentimental beasts are all the same,
Stupid and loving, quick to kiss or cry;
That dragon last week, with his comfy game
Of burning love-words on the midnight sky;
Or any unicornish creature:
Two heads or just one eye.
I wish they wouldn't come and slobber,
For
I'm through with oddities of nature.

A CHILD'S GARDEN

I'm sure I can't remember where, but some
Where in this jungle I have lost the key
That locks the door of Grandfather's walled garden
Where he and I, before he died, would play,

And he would sing about the funny sun
That circled over the garden every day.
But then he died. I didn't know a thing
Of what a grown-up would have done, and so

I ran away when April ate him up,
Our dog. And now the door is shut, and just
The walls are all I see, and sometimes I
Don't know if there's a garden there at all.

The animals just look at me. I bit
A rat to death three days ago and ate him.
A tiger has been padding all today
Behind me, and I cannot sleep at all.

I cannot sleep at all, and what is worse
Yesterday I tried to talk again
Just like I did with Grampa, but my voice
Was only grunts. I made no words at all.

For Jay Lewis

CAROL

The Christ was born
On Christmas day
In Bethlehem,
The Gospels say.

The manger warmed
Both man and beast
For pagans filled
The inns with feast.

Good angels watched
The Christ be born
And charmed the air
With harps till morn.

The warmth of cows
Around the hay
Kept cold from God
As there He lay.

The animals
Knew God was there
Because a light
Was in the air.

When morning came
The Christ arose
And was a man,
Couleur de rose.

THREE STANZAS

It is a sudden birth
That in this moon emergence now
Ascends among the textures of the wind.
It builds a darkness full of tiny leaves
  Whose voices like the wink of bells
  Make music of our motions.

That burden falls, and all
The heavy movement is at end.
Now water flows where other sounds are gone,
And slowly through the underbrush the flood
  Seeps up and chases frightened deer
  To hilly farming country.

The barn is burning, o,
The barn is burning on the hill,
The cattle low and blunder in their stalls,
The horses scream and hurl their burning manes,
  The barn is burning where the night
  Sweetens the seed of fire.

Those several times she cleaved my dark,
Silver and homeless, I from sleep
Rose up, and tried to touch or mark
That storied personage with deep
Unmotivated love. My days were full,
My halting days were full of rage,
Resisting in my heart the pull
Toward reverence or pilgrimage.
But now this blinding sheeted bird
Or goddess stood at my bed's head,
Demanding worship, and no word
But honoring the steadfast dead.

IUVENES DUM SUMUS

Bowing he asks her the favor,
    Blushing she answers she will,
Waltzing they turn through the ballroom,
    Swift in their skill.

Blinder than buffers of autumn,
    Deaf but to music's delight,
They dance like the puppets of music
    All through the night.

Out of the ball they come dancing
    And into the marketing day,
Waltzing through ignorant traffic,
    Bound to be gay.

Suddenly now in the city
    Her dress is bedraggled and worn,
His suit while he waltzes is ancient,
    Ragged and torn.

They slacken and stoop, they are tired,
    They walk in the weather of pain;
Now wrinkles dig into their faces,
    Sharp as the rain.

They walk by identical houses
    And enter the one that they know.
They are old, and their children like houses
    Stand in a row.

2. *Love Is Like Sounds*

LOVE IS LIKE SOUNDS

Late snow fell this early morning of spring.
At dawn I rose from bed, restless, and looked
Out of the window, to wonder if there the snow
Fell outside your bedroom, and you watching.

I played my game of solitaire. The cards
Came out the same the third time through the deck.
The game was stuck. I threw the cards together,
And watched the snow that could not do but fall.

Love is like sounds, whose last reverberations
Hang on the leaves of strange trees, on mountains
More distant than the farthest continent,
Where the snow hangs still in the middle of the air.

The old must watch us as we walk the streets,
And ghosts of flesh must summon in their brains
    The autumns of a fallen past,
The lovers' woods in which no tree remains.

And then the memory of bits of leaf
Caught in the loosened hair; by heavy seas
    The wind that rasped across their skin,
And all the body's changing cruelties,

Must make them hate us as we walk the streets,
Hand in hand and brushing hip to thigh,
    And they must think we love, and know
That they can only watch and wait to die.

When skin hangs loose upon your shaken limbs,
Remember love you feared when you were young.
    Then read this on a weary night,
And roll these vowels on a shrunken tongue.

AFTERNOON

My mouse, my girl in gray, I speak to her;
One day in autumn I will wander through
A closed amusement park, past shacks that were
A moment since the palaces of rue
Where gaudy prizes hung along the stand
Seduced the quarter from no gambler's hand.

And there will be the boarded House of Fun,
And leaves will tumble past the Whirl-O-Ride.
I will move on, content as anyone,
And then will see her walking to my side,
My mouse, my girl. She will not speak, but smile,
And we will walk together, for a while.

SEPTEMBER ODE

And now September burns the careful tree
That builds each year the leaf and bark again
With solemn care and rounded certainty
That nothing lives which seasons do not mend.

But we were strangers in that formal wood
Those years ago, and we have grown to change,
Ignorant of the fury of the blood,
And we have tasted what is new and strange.

This new September's pilgrimage is made,
Remembering that season of the mind
When we were Tamburlaines of leaf and shade
And Alexanders of the lusty wind.

But only seasons spin around the tree
In winter thick and summer narrow bark;
The person learns a changing cruelty;
Possessions cumber us from going back.

Only the young are really pitiable
Who walk from high school past my cluttered room,
Who live in last night's party, and who tell
What happened in the darkened living room.

That innocence is only negative
And innocence is only not to know
That all intensity is curative
In the disease of love we undergo.

This room is cluttered with the truth of years,
Possessions of the unreturning blood.
And innocence possesses only fear
Of parting from the comfort of the wood.

Wealthy with love and fruitful memory,
I pity only those who have no guilt.
It is the structure of complicity,
The monument experience has built.

The tree is burning on the autumn noon
That builds each year the leaf and bark again.
Though frost will strip it raw and barren soon,
The rounding season will restore and mend.

Yet people are not mended, but go on,
Accumulating memory and love.
And so the wood we used to know is gone,
Because the years have taught us that we move.

We have moved on, the Tamburlaines of then,
To different Asias of our plundering.
And though we sorrow not to know again
A land or face we loved, yet we are king.

The young are never robbed of innocence
But given gold of love and memory.
We live in wealth whose bounds exceed our sense,
And when we die are full of memory.

Tonight the snow is falling; city sky
Is domed and hollowed by the flaking light.
The snows of this day powder and float by
To sink on clean parabolas of white.
My day is joy, and all the paths of snow
Are singing where I go,
Where brilliant angels soften on my hair,
And salve the brick and iron of the Square.

Today, the last of January, she
Has come to twenty-one; those years ago
At Morris Cove in wintry poverty
The child was born tonight who was to grow
So soon into a girl whose gentleness
And beauty were to bless
The mixed compartments of my character
With new delight, for utter love of her.

All of the world was fractured to delight
Five years ago July, when she, sixteen,
Colored the sky with love and thought it light.
Then I was gay, though I had always been
Morose and comical and schoolboy sad
And yearning to be mad.
But when three years of love had rounded out,
I said that love was over, and no doubt.

A spoken motive is a spoken lie,
I learned, because I knew or thought I knew
A plenteous stock of worthy reasons why
I had to force the ugly ending through.
But then I learned that deeps of character
Erupted hate of her,
And for no reason that a man could see
I hated what had loved and sheltered me.

Perversity and loss now chill the air,
And gulls of snow fade down from middle flight.
I walk, and only find a shelter where
I speak these words against the flaking night.
And now I wish my birthday wish for you,
And pray the wish come true.
"Oh, may you walk beneath a friendly sun
Though human things desert you one by one;

"Along the huddled Cambridge streets, the snow
Sifts down upon the living and the dead
And on the river struggling free to flow.
It makes no difference; joy fills up my head.
I do not understand this circumstance
When snow-gulls laugh and dance
Along the Cambridge streets, but it is true:
May all your life explain this joy to you."

SONG

No more the Tamburlaine
   To your Zenocrate,
I have renounced my reign
   Your husbandman to be,
      Your husbandman to be.

Here where the forest is
   A roof for simple men,
Each farmer loves what's his,
   And we learn love again,
      And we learn love again.

In herding swine and sheep,
   Not emperors today,
We love as hard and deep,
   But love a different way,
      But love a different way.

Where once I conquered you
   In armored metaphor,
Today with figures few
   I sing those songs no more,
      I sing those songs no more,

But sing of mountain grass,
   Of things perhaps banal,
But things that will not pass—
   A summer's pastoral,
      A summer's pastoral.

VALENTINE

Chipmunks jump, and
Greensnakes slither.
Rather burst than
Not be with her.

Bluebirds fight, but
Bears are stronger.
We've got fifty
Years or longer.

Hoptoads hop, but
Hogs are fatter.
Nothing else but
Us can matter.

3. Old Home Day

OLD HOME DAY
WILMOT, NEW HAMPSHIRE

Man to man remembers when
Bat and ball would ring this plain,
Fifty years ago, before
The batter's box washed out in rain.

Behind the eyeless, staring lid,
And in the pucker of a mouth,
Gullied meadows cave together
Crumpled in the latest drouth.

No mouth will answer, though I ask
Of dying men or dying earth,
For what unheard-of harvest does
The land lie seedless, begging birth?

i

October wind
Is Northern Spy,
Ranges through
The long sky.

The day is filled
With flying seed,
Flotsam of
The dead weed.

ii

The drifted snow
Warms the farm,
Haymow low
In dark barn.

Icicles
Hang from the shed,
High-piled quilts
On feather bed.

iii

In April, mud
Begins to crack,
And chattering clouds
Of birds fly back.

The creek is full
  And the bear, awake,
Stumbles past
  The rising lake.

iv
Summer rain
  Wets the hay,
The window blank
  With the gray day.

The tie-up clean,
  The hens fed,
Today is rest,
  And work ahead.

The maples of Connecticut
  In dry October breezes flare
    All shades of orange, shades of red.
There is my home, but I have not
  For two Octobers rested there,
    Nor the red maples visited.

The English autumn pales the trees
  With yellow fog to ornament
    This island jewel of a queen.
As morbid as a slow disease
  October makes its faint descent
    Toward winter's rainy quarantine.

Another year and I will be
  Returned to where the seasons are,
    Each delicate compartment shut.
Then I will watch the maple tree
  That tells position like a star:
    October and Connecticut.

NEW ENGLAND NOVEMBER

In that New Haven house
Where laughing relatives
Perform the family jokes
And all the family lives,

Where turkey roasted whole,
Potatoes, turnips, peas,
Onions and Brussels sprouts,
And globes of Holland cheese,

Where pumpkin, apple, mince,
And seven kinds of pie,
Plum pudding, cake, and nuts
Astound and satisfy;

Or in that northern house
Where two old people stay,
Valley'd between red hills
That burn the sky away,

And stuff their cellar full
Of food won by the hand
In years of laboring
On the New Hampshire land;

That country now is full
Of fire and plenteousness,
And pride blesses the land;
The land comes back to bless.

Oxford, England

JAMAICA

Nothing is taller than a royal palm
Or straighter than its swelling, waning trunk
Crowned by the fronds that rattle in the wind.
Country of grasses, thronging sugar cane,
And the green thickets of the young bamboo,
No where is quite so spendthrift of its green.

The market air is thick, and the complaints
Of beggars multiply among the mules.
Along the windy Caribbean shore
The smell of dunder from a factory,
Refuse of sugar, saturates the air
Until the inland plain begins to climb.

Acres of cane, white Squire upon his horse,
His foreman by his side; on hillsides steer,
In other valleys rows of coconuts;
On top a hill, the Georgian great-house stands,
Built for defense two hundred years ago,
Where Squire and Mistress rule behind thick walls.

Farther, the cockpit country, where the slaves
Escaped when England took the land from Spain,
And where a tribe still squats, the wild Maroons,
Not subject to Her Majesty's appointed.
Here dead men live in silver cottonwoods,
And it is called "the land of look-behind."

Over the island heavy with its green
Whose unpremeditated growth is food,
A long Atlantic wind gives canopy.
Upon the wind, great herds of vultures ride
Over the bristling acreage of grcen,
Where there is always something which is dead.

BAMBOO

"Wales"
    Falmouth
        Jamaica, B.W.I.

In clumps like grass
    By the road near Wales,
By the muddy river,
    Bamboo prevails.

Big winds uproot
    Fifty together,
A whole clump
    In a bad weather.

The young bamboo,
    Metallic green,
Spreads at the top
    A feathered screen:

Green paint on steel
    Of stalk; and higher,
Lighter fronds
    As fine as wire.

At tropical Wales
    The light is made
By types of green
    In the hot shade,

And from a hill
  The earth is masses
Of cane, bamboo,
  And other grasses.

Even the dignity of Christ
Whose churches were clean white
Here sinks.
The sixty-mile-an-hour tourist thinks
How quaint the rack
And ruin which attack
The limbs of Christ,
The Christian light.
Where once a hundred farmers came to pray,
Today twelve relics sit
At some odd time of day
When a fatigued young man can say his bit.
He has three parishes
Whose people are devout
But scarcely forty-five in counting out.
Yet down the road,
The Roman lady, à la mode,
With wooden-shingled flying buttresses,
Builds new
Her local imitation Notre-Dame,
Where city people on vacation come
To celebrate the garments of the true.

The high blue air of August stands today
Over the heavy hay,
Whose facets now the small winds multiply.
But the dead houses cannot take the hay.
The cellar holes that populate the hills,
And the abandoned farms the roads pass by,
Only the spider fills.
The tall hay slopes to the earth each year,

While pink motels appear
With rusted signs on every wall.
The labor and the land together fall.
The rush of cars
Is all the noise that jars
Immobile earth, unbroken, thin, and old.
A crowd of pines and maples spreads along
Acres of ancient garden gone to wood,
And where a farmhouse stood,
There is a sign of something wrong—
A maple touched in part by blight or cold
So that one branch is red, on a green tree.
Death of a part is agony;
So far one branch is red on this green tree.

4. Matter of Fact

MATTER OF FACT

No Deposit.   No Return.
  Said the bottle dead of beer.
Toughly by small things we learn
  Courage in this hemisphere,
Bleak and honest to affirm
A single independent term.

It only hurts me when I laugh.
  Said the hunter crucified.
I'm not Jesus Christ by half,
  So keep all weapons from my side
Or you'll take a dead man's curse;
Life is hell, but death is worse.

In the caves of the Dordogne
  Paleolithic doctors made
Records with their flint and stone
  Of the slogans of the trade:
Strike the big bulls in the heart;
Leave the pregnant cows apart.

Shoot these old gray hairs, she said,
  But spare your country's flag! He thought—
Then Stonewall Jackson went ahead
  And ordered Barbara Frietchie shot,
Which was unchivalric, and
Suited to the time's demand.

The hairy fetch of felt disease,
  Which glories in its brutal name,
Eats anguish like a Stilton cheese

And spreads, in process, crafty blame,
Until no person fouled by it
Can keep the savors separate.

Dillinger the killer died
   In a theater lobby when
One who slept at his own side
   Squealed his name to the G-Men.
His final utterance was heard
To be a single dirty word.

Chinese Gordon sat alone
   When the Mahdi broke the door;
He fired twice, and did not groan
   When they speared him to the floor.
Two he shot before he died
Flanked him dead on either side.

Though the name of failure bray
   Like a donkey in despair,
Who must weep that jacks betray
   In the dark the darling mare,
We shall take our failures up
And drink them down from the full cup.

It only hurts me when I bray,
   Chinese Gordon said, and died.
Disease is hairier today,
   Said Barbara Frietchie crucified.
But she added from the hearse,
Life is hell, but death is worse.

Dillinger spoke, and doctors drew
    Records of what the killer said,
Where Stonewall Jackson came to view
    Six pregnant cows untimely dead,
Upon whose sides one could discern
No Deposit.   No Return.

You play the cop, and I'm the robber type.
　　I know of many a crime
　　For which I should do time;
I wear—inside—the horizontal stripe.

All of your impulse rushes to undo
　　Poor me for stealing pans
　　Or old tobacco cans,
Or blowing up a bank, or wanting to.

Ambush in alleys, sneaky midnight raids—
　　You always nearly win,
　　But luck belongs to sin:
I learn of secret passageways from maids.

When I go West, you wear a marshal's star,
　　Persistent as a curse,
　　And when I steal a purse,
A note inside says, "I know who you are."

In Paris with a black beret, I sell
　　Disgusting pictures to
　　Americans, but you
Appear disguised among my clientele.

In England I am awfully on my guard.
　　With a new mustache, I live
　　In Soho as a spiv,
Until you drop around from Scotland Yard.

In far Antarctica, with Admiral Byrd,
    I feel secure, though chilly,
    Till toward me, with a billy,
An outsized penguin lumbers from the herd.

Let observation with extensive view
Watch the blind staggers of the kangaroo.
The chipmunk hiccups, and the tall giraffe
Eats awnings from high houses for a laugh.
The mole, the rabbit, and the fat hedgehog
Dance on the quarters of the snoring dog.
Those gaudy elephants are nasty drunks
And take to whipping piglets with their trunks.
The lion lurches, and the bear recites
The poems that he very seldom writes.
A terrible noise in the menagerie:
Delirium tremens of the chickadee.
But worst of all, a drunken kitten sits
And tears a drunken goat to tiny bits.

I gave my girl a chocolate bar,
    Chum-jee, gum-blox.
She said, "That's going awfully far,
    Chum-jee, gum-blox."
  And I replied, as quick's a frog,
  "Able   Baker   Charlie   Dog,
    Easy   Fox."

I took away her chocolate bar,
    Chum-jee, gum-blox.
She said, "I really wanted more,
    Chum-jee, gum-blox."
  And I replied, "You fat old hog,
  Able   Baker   Charlie   Dog,
    Easy   Fox."

She greatly groaned, and then she cried,
    "Chum-jee! Gum-blox!"
She said, "Oh, when did you decide?
    Chum-jee? Gum-blox?"
  And I replied, to lay a fog,
  "Able   Baker   Charlie   Dog,
    Easy   Fox."

She took herself some miles away,
    Chum-jee, gum-blox,
And on a cliff she paused to say,
    "Chum-jee, gum-blox."
  The cliff replied, "We're all agog,
  Able   Baker   Charlie   Dog,
    Easy   Fox."

She jumped and fell so awfully far,
　　Chum-jee, gum-blox,
It took a lifetime till the jar,
　　Chum-jee, gum-blox.
　Three vultures sighed, "O Gog! Magog!
　Able! Baker! Charlie! Dog!
　　　Easy! Fox!"

MARY MARGARET MC BRIDE INTERVIEWS
DANDY, *THE POET*

I write, dear Madame, out of pain,
    And into pleasure,
Scanning my days that I attain
    Accurate measure.

I write, dear Madame, on account
    Of law and order,
That no bad sentiment surmount
    A guarded border.

I write, dear Madame, for the pose,
    Which is the matter;
If he does not, a poet goes
    Mad, like a hatter.

I put my hat upon my head
And walk'd into the Strand;
And there I met another man
Whose hat was in his hand.

The only trouble with the man
Whom I had met was that,
As he walked swinging both his arms,
His head was in his hat.

Finesse be first, whose elegance deplores
All things save beauty, and the swinging doors;
Whose cleverness in writing verse is just
Exceeded by his lack of taste and lust;
Who lives off lady lovers of his verse
And thanks them by departing with their purse;
Who writes his verse in order to amaze,
To win the Pulitzer, or *Time*'s sweet praise;
Who will endure a moment, and then pass,
As hopeless as an olive in his glass.

Dullard be second, as he always will,
From lack of brains as well as lack of skill.
Expert in some, and dilettante in all
The ways of making poems gasp and fall,
He teaches at a junior college where
He's recognized as Homer's son and heir.
Respectable, brown-suited, it is he
Who represents on forums poetry,
And argues to protect the libeled Muse,
Who'd tear his flimsy tongue out, could she choose.

His opposite is anarchistic *Bomb*,
Who writes a manifesto with aplomb.
Revolt! Revolt! No matter why or when,
It's novelty, old novelty again.
Yet *Bomb* if read intently may reveal
A talent not to murder but to steal;
First from old *Gone*, whose fragmentary style
Disguised his sawdust Keats a little while;

And now from one who writes at very best
What ne'er was thought and much the less expressed.

Lucre be next, who takes to poetry
The businessman he swore he would not be.
Anthologies and lecture tours and grants
Create a solvency which disenchants.
He writes his poems now to suit his purse,
Short-lined and windy, and reserves his curse
For all the little magazines so fine
That offer only fifty cents a line.
He makes his money, certainly, to write,
But writes for money. Such is appetite.

Of *Mucker* will I tell, who tries to show
He is a kind of poet men don't know.
To shadow box at literary teas
And every girl at Bennington to seize,
To talk of baseball rather than of Yeats,
To drink straight whisky while the bard creates—
This is his pose, and so his poems seem
Incongruous in proving life a dream.
Some say, with Freud, that *Mucker* has a reason
For acting virile in and out of season.

Scoundrel be last. Be deaf, be dumb, be blind,
Who writes satiric verses on his kind.

5. The Strangers

THE SLEEPING GIANT
(A HILL, SO NAMED, IN HAMDEN, CONNECTICUT)

The whole day long, under the walking sun
That poised an eye on me from its high floor,
Holding my toy beside the clapboard house
I looked for him, the summer I was four.

I was afraid the waking arm would break
From the loose earth and rub against his eyes
A fist of trees, and the whole country tremble
In the exultant labor of his rise;

Then he with giant steps in the small streets
Would stagger, cutting off the sky, to seize
The roofs from house and home because we had
Covered his shape with dirt and planted trees;

And then kneel down and rip with fingernails
A trench to pour the enemy Atlantic
Into our basin, and the water rush,
With the streets full and all the voices frantic.

That was the summer I expected him.
Later the high and watchful sun instead
Walked low behind the house, and school began,
And winter pulled a sheet over his head.

When it is truly the moon that he sees
in the dead of sleep, then the tall night-mair
shakes wolf-bane on him, and his breath hurries

and she spreads the cover of her black hair,
feathered with carrion birds, and tasting
in sleep like the looming of change somewhere.

He twists in his dream at first, not knowing
what is becoming of him. Then he is
content to lie beneath the slow changing

that starts from every pore. He finishes
with the curved nails and the curl of the lip
from the eyeteeth that perceptibly rise

pointed white. Virgins, despair. His gambit
of finding her whitely asleep, sweet to
morsel the jaws, unrecking of his rip,

has never lacked. After, the fat hero,
he takes his time in wholly rehearsing
details of her flavor. Evil be thou

his good. In his entire, thorough-going
depravity of frightfully evil
wishes, he is consistently charming.

Yet, it is done with props. Now, versatile,
the hair falls out, the long eyeteeth loosen,
and he straightens to enter the hotel

for breakfast, where a girl from Washington
waits to be entertained. Since he requires
the correct light and costume for his fun,

and good timing, she is quite safe. Desires,
to be fulfilled, are made theatrical.
So he eats toast, and quietly admires

the meat of her rump, and thinks of the call
of the night-mair another month, looming,
to assume his werewolf suit, assume all

relish of evil, wolf in wolf's clothing.

At Delphi where the eagles climb
Over Parnassus' naked head
I saw the burden of the dead,
  Perfected out of time.

I met a donkey and a man
Who carted olive branches through
The marble wastes where little grew
  And once great runners ran.

The temple where the priestess told
Young Oedipus whom he would kill
Lay dissipated on the hill,
  Where grass grew faint as mold.

No priestess spoke. I heard one sound.
The donkey's sure and nerveless plod
Past ruined columns of a god
  Made dactyls on the ground.

TO THE LOUD WIND

Mime the loud wind in pain—
The worded room will yield
Your canny agony
Not excellence nor will.

Dreams and asylums build
No words of sounding luck.
The metronome of guilt
Does sums behind the lock.

A maiden intellect
Sits safe indoors and still
When loud complexity
Thunders electrical.

Not subtlety nor guilt
But will made concentrate
Shouts the loud wind to fill
The worded intellect.

Over my bed
   My father stood,
Fixed in the stead
   Of abstract God.

I swore to build
   A place of play
Without a willed
   Authority.

Today I stand
   Above a son,
Though I had planned
   Catch as catch can.

Over my bed
   Last night there stood
The form I dread
   Of father God.

By an over-shape
   Still we are ruled,
And no escape
   From the fixed world.

IN MEMORY OF AUGUSTA HALL

1. HER DEATH

Now close her eyes, for all her breath is gone.
They will not open up to pain again.

For years the crab has fed between her bones
That took her final breath now, all at once.

Self-conscious of decay, we suffer on
Until our selves are willing to be done.

Now let her down: her body let us bless
That moved from birth through beauty into this.

2. HER MEMORY

We who waited on her bed
Keep the joking words she said,
And our love preserves intact
Word and photograph and fact.

Gathered every year, we may,
Christmas and Thanksgiving Day,
Resurrect familial dead
With the breaking of our bread.

Men retain the image of
Persons whom they wholly love,
And until we die like her
For a while she will endure.

When we die her life will be
Dead to human memory,
But her courage and her wit
First survive her death a bit.

THE STRANGERS

O garden of strangers, declensions
  Of face repeating face,
I walked through the rushing of flowers
  To meet your race.

None of you sheltered a signal
  Of perfect small decay
But fixed at the crux of the summer
  A summer day.

I saw no design in your garden
  But what was everywhere;
Your movement was liquid, and easy
  The pollened air.

I wanted to enter your garden
  And join your single state,
But rank upon rank of your sameness
  Secured the gate.

The Pioneers, the Cat Men, and the Wolves,
 Leaning together under a hissing light,
In argot plan their conduct through the streets,
 Their violence upon the easy night.

Their studded belts, their leather jackets show
 Their wish to be alike and to be led,
Whether on motorcycles in a pack
 Or each in turn upon a single bed.

They crowd the highways with their mortal skill,
 The litter of their deaths, their games of speed;
In love with death, and loving nothing else,
 Their only conversation is the deed.

The wilder ones are made unique in print
 When it is only killing which delights,
But tiny fretful crimes for most of them
 Are adequate to glut their appetites.

Their small aggressions aggregate a war.
 Their random conduct signifies attack.
The Pioneers, the Cat Men, and the Wolves
 Gather within the cities they will sack.

My history extends
Where moved my tourist hands,
Who traveled on their own
Without a helping brain.

My hands that domineered
My body lacking mind
Pulled me around the globe
Like any country rube.

No more automaton,
Smarter and settled down,
I choose to move my hands
Which way my will extends.

I marvel now to mark
The geographic work
Done by my brainless touch
On every foreign latch.

In active consciousness
I now rehearse those trips
Which I no longer take
And only partly took.

A STUDY OF HISTORY

The old man said,
Although a house may fall
It does no harm at all,
That it is dead,
As long as you and you and you aren't dead.

Houses go wrong.
He starves that took the rent,
But we set up a tent
And get along;
We manage it, and live our lives along.

A country too
Like Nineveh or Tyre
Can be consumed by fire,
If just a few
Survive to make the most of being few.

They live in dread
That cherish an excess.
There is no happiness,
The old man said,
Except in understanding things, he said.

ON A BIRTHDAY

Now I am twenty-five.
I struggle to survive

The pain of vanity.
I pray the will may be

More powerful, that I
May myself magnify.

The will is enemy
To the mere vanity

That seeks small gain, to beat
What local skill it meet,

Acedia, despair,
Enclose whose poisoned air,

Within whose closure hide
The sweets of suicide.

Not all desire is vain;
The will exhorts the brain

To make a permanence
Of mortal utterance.

I pray for time and place
To shape my changing face

And loose intelligence
By will to excellence,

So that from death will be
Preserved some part of me.

In hate of death I make
These words for my own sake.

THE BODY POLITIC

I shot my friend to save my country's life,
And when the happy bullet struck him dead,
I was saluted by the drum and fife
Corps of a high school, while the traitor bled.

I never thought until I pulled the trigger
But that I did the difficult and good.
I thought republics stood for something bigger,
For the mind of man, as Plato said they stood.

So when I heard the duty they assigned,
Shooting my friend seemed only sanity;
To keep disorder from the state of mind
Was mental rectitude, it seemed to me.

The audience dispersed. I felt depressed.
I went to where my orders issued from,
But the right number on the street was just
A rickety old house, vacant and dumb.

I tried to find the true address, but where?
Nobody told me what I really wanted;
Just secretaries sent me here and there
To other secretaries. I was daunted.

Poor Fred. His presence will be greatly missed
By children and by cronies by the score.
The State (I learn too late) does not exist;
Man lives by love, and not by metaphor.

6. Exiles

EXILE

Each of us waking to the window's light
Has found the curtains changed, our pictures gone;
Our furniture has vanished in the night
And left us to an unfamiliar dawn.
Even the contours of our room are strange
And everything is change.
Waking, our minds construct of memory
What figure stretched beside us, or what voice
Shouted to pull us from our luxury—
And all the mornings leaning to our choice.

To put away—both child and murderer—
The toys we played with just a month ago,
That wisdom come, and make our moving sure,
Began our exile with our lust to grow.
(Remembering a train I tore apart,
Because it knew my heart.)
We move and move, but our perversity
Betrays us into love of what is lost.
We search our minds for childhood, and we see
Only the parting struggle and its cost.

Not only from the intellectual child
Time has removed us, but unyieldingly
Cuts down the groves in which our Indians filed
And where the sleep of pines was mystery.
(I walked the streets of where I lived and grew,
And all the streets were new.)
The room of love is always rearranged.
Someone has torn the corner of a chair

83

So that the past we cultivate is changed,
The scene deprived by an intruding tear.

Exiled by death from men that we have known,
We are betrayed again by years, and try
To call them back and clothe the barren bone,
Not to admit a man can ever die.
(A boy who talked and read and grew with me,
Fell from a maple tree.)
But we are still alone, who love the dead,
And always miss their action's character,
Trapped in our cells of living, visited
By no sweet ghosts, by no sad men that were.

In years, and in the numbering of space
Thousands of miles from what we grew to know,
We stray like paper blown from place to place,
Impelled by every element to go.
(I think of haying on an August day,
Forking the stacks of hay.)
We can remember trees and attitudes
That foreign landscapes do not imitate;
They grow distinct within the interludes
Of memory beneath a stranger state.

The favorite toy was banished, and our act
Was banishment of the self; then growing, we
Murdered the girls we loved, for our love lacked
Self-knowledge of its real perversity.
(I loved her, but I told her I did not,
And grew, and then forgot.)
It was mechanical, and in our age,
That cruelty should be our way of speech;

Our movement is a single pilgrimage,
Never returning; action does not teach.

In isolation from our present love
We spell her out in daily memory,
Thinking these images we practice move
On human avenues across a sea.
(All day I see her simple figure stand,
Out of the reach of hand.)
Each door and window is a spectral frame
In which her ghost is for the moment found.
Each lucky scrap of paper bears her name,
And half-heard phrases imitate its sound.

Imagining, by exile kept from fact,
We build of distance mental rock and tree,
And make of memory creative act,
Persons and worlds no waking eye can see.
(From lacking her, I built her new again,
And loved the image then.)
The manufactured country is so green
The eyes of sleep are blinded by its shine;
We spend our lust in that imagined scene
But never wake to cross its borderline.

No man can knock his human fist upon
The door built by his mind, or hear the voice
He meditated come again if gone;
We live outside the country of our choice.
Leaning toward harvest, fullness as our end,
Our habits will not mend.
Our humanness betrays us to the cage
Within whose limits each is free to walk,

But where no man can hear our prayers or rage,
And none of us can break the walls to talk.

Exiled by years, by death the present end,
By worlds that must remain unvisited,
And by the wounds that growing does not mend,
We are as solitary as the dead,
Wanting to king it in that perfect land
We make and understand.
And in this world whose pattern is unmade,
Phases of splintered light and shapeless sand,
We shatter through our motions and evade
Whatever hand might reach and touch our hand.

Newdigate Prize Poem, Oxford, 1952

JE SUIS UNE TABLE

It has happened suddenly,
by surprise, in an arbor,
or while drinking good coffee,
after speaking, or before,

that I dumbly inhabit
a density; in language
nothing is to prevent it,
nothing to retain an edge.

Arrant ignorance presents,
later, words for a function,
but it is the weak pretense
of speech, by mere convention,

and there is nothing at all
but the work of years, nothing
to relieve on principle
now this intense thickening.

Habit of conversation
(thickly turned thing) may make none.

1

Bentley is hanged. Though Bevan raged at Fyfe,
Sir David jerked those stupid muscles loose,
Those knees to water. Bentley lost his life,
His mouth ajar, dumb as the hangman's noose.

He had not fired the shot that is fulfilled.
His partner Craig, at sixteen years secure,
Shot the policeman for whose death is killed
Bentley at nineteen, not a murderer.

The simple robbery, a London store
One morning in the easy London rain,
And pounds enough to live a year or more
For little risk: small risk and a great gain.

But nothing worked according to the plan.
A watchman brought policemen with a shout,
And on across the rainy roofs they ran,
Until, with Bentley caught, Craig shot it out.

My kinship is with Bentley who is hanged.
He blundered dumbly into sin and death
And did not know how sharp the worm was fanged
That spoke of ease, and took his easy breath.

There is no comfort in my guilty skull.
It pulses with his ignorant decease,
Rhyme of appointed death, and knows my will
Empty of all but its infirmities.

Both guilt and guilty ignorance of sin,
Be done. No action mattered at the time,
But now, to prove the error, I begin
To make confession of each narrow crime.

No Parliament or pardon can efface
Or any kind decree or law amend
The simple lie that rots the lying face,
But smooths an amorous day's, or poem's end.

Long dalliance with the frantic and the sore,
Dishonesty of motive, hidden doubt,
Perverse embrace of what I most abhor—
For mortal punishment my sins cry out.

I climb the scaffold with the killer's friend,
And feel the knot that leans against my ear.
He had not guessed, nor I, that it would end,
The body swinging from a sky of fear.

NO STORY

Now I grow big with her
and she not here
but lost on victory and tossing where
benighted whiteness shelters her from harm—
yet guilty to the million hints of fame.
And all the mourning dances she might wear
depend upon the growing she has sworn
unbearable, and I
have borne but with perversity.

An image mints itself again
of the white night, and tired bodies torn
with rocking to a tune
whose rhyme is stale and moving to defeat,
defeat and contradictions of the flesh.
But there was momentary night
and the tiredness of love.
How we are fragmentary
and have no story.

THE WORLD, THE TIMES

The habit of these years is constant choice.
Each act, each moment, is political.
Enormous power responds to one man's voice.
The President and Cabinet are on call.
Great freedom walks in us, and we command
The universe forever to expand.

The world, the times, the country, and the age
Maneuver toward eventuality.
We wait the coming; maybe in a rage
Great conquerors will come, our leaders be,
To take the generations into war
Until we men and women are no more;

Or maybe at some Easter we will find
A martyr who by absence wins the earth,
Who walked in life before us who were blind,
And whom we will await in second birth;
So live in holy darkness, and be sure
Our souls if not our bodies are secure.

However may the future be disguised,
I praise the moment, when no world is made.
Anarchy works to kill the civilized
And nothing will prevent a mortal raid
Except defense with violence again
Within the minds of many single men.

Now men are Persian in their ease, and fling
All difficulties out, for the freed man
Believes no good or ill in anything,

But loves his minute's pleasure, or what can
So glorify his days that they will be
Productive of his own security.

There's no security except the grave;
There's much belief in what does not exist.
All that is excellent is hard to save,
Since every man is partly anarchist.
We live by choice, and choose with every act
That form or chaos move from mind to fact.

I name an age of choice and discontent
Whose emblem is "the difficult to choose."
Each man is free to act, but his intent
Must circumscribe what he may not refuse.
Each moment is political, and we
Are clothed in nothing but mortality.

THE TREE

Now ornamental winter tends the tree
With golden angels and a shepherd's star,
Above the pausing Magi, as they see,

Ahead among the cotton snow not far,
The stable where their journey is to go,
Where carven Jesus and His Mother are.

Like them I find the days and months too slow;
Too slow the minutes, waiting for a birth.
Today a year, another child will know

An ornamental tree, a pot of earth,
These silver birds and angels flossed with gold—
Pretense of gold, and innocence of dearth.

New fingers will explore the crèche, and hold
Camel or cow indifferent in the hand,
While past the window winter will be cold.

From cold, which any mind can understand,
The year will turn to spring. And then the tree,
Disornamented, raw, will come to stand

Upon the summit of bald Calvary,
Broken and crossed to bear the weight and span
Of Jesus dying in His agony

Upon the trunk of birth like every man.

THE BLIND

When I was made a man
I comprehended that
Complicity began
The months my mother sat
To hold me at her breast.
The rude unseeking need
Involved me with the rest
Of the contingent breed.
Complicity began,
Yet distance is as fit;
Now I am more a man,
And I am separate.

Men who despair attain
No honest balm, but learn
The tricks of staying sane:
The eyes that never turn,
No matter what the view,
The face that must obey
The uncompelling, true
Conventions of the day,
The mind that must insist,
Though lacking contact, yet,
That other minds exist
Not wholly separate.

The blind upon the blind,
Who nuzzle for their ease,
Are seeking till they find
(Said Aristophanes)
Their body's counterpart,

By a divine misdeed
Divided heart from heart
And left with this great need.
The soul that from our urge
Spouted to build a man
Must always try to merge
With where his life began,

To reach, across the space,
A momentary point,
Where face presses on face
And character is joint.
The passionate display
Will reach bewilderment,
Self-conscious of decay,
Of the vacant years spent,
Of distances to go
To touch a mind with mind,
Until he comes to know
That the blind upon the blind

Only conceive the blind.

AN ELEGY FOR WESLEY WELLS
DEAD MARCH 9, 1953

Against the clapboards and the windowpanes
Whines the loud March with rain and heavy wind,
In dark New Hampshire where his widow wakes.
She cannot sleep. The familiar length is gone.
I stand alone among the English crowds
And think across the clamorous Atlantic
To where the farm lies hard against the foot
Of Ragged Mountain, underneath Kearsarge.
The sea between is shrouded up in storm
That heaves the carcasses of burly ships
Against the rocks of England, and I know
The storm and hooded wind of equinox
Bluster against New England's bolted door
Across the sea, and set the signals out
Eastport to Block Island. I hear the wind
Alone and far from him, my mother's father,
Buried this afternoon those miles away.
Here, in the crowded place his people left
Three centuries ago,
I speak his name against the beating sea.

The farmer dead, his horse will run to fat.
He will go lame and whinny from his stall.
The lambing spring will come again, but now,
Lacking his gentle hands, the small will die
If the new night is cold when they are born.
Where the tall corn designed a labyrinth,
And he kept farmer's hold with mind or tool,
Scrub brush and weed will raise their common heads.
His dogs will whimper through the webby barn,

Where spiders close his tools in a pale gauze
And wait for flies. The nervous woodchuck now
Will waddle plumply through the world of weeds,
Eating wild peas, as if he owned the land,
And the fat hedgehog rob the apple trees.
When next October's frosts harden the earth,
And fasten in the year's catastrophe,
The farm will lie like driftwood,
The farmer dead, and deep in his carved earth.

His father was a smith. He helped him out,
Then worked at Andover and Potter Place
In general stores, and liked the jobs because
They gave him scope to talk with every kind.
In nineteen-hundred-two he married her
Whom years by he had met in Sunday school,
And worked her father's farm. The land was good,
But all the farms had slumped for forty years.
Before the Civil War the land was used,
And railroads came to all the villages;
Before the war, a man with land was rich;
He cleared a thousand or two thousand acres,
Burning the timber, stacking up the stones,
And cultivated all his acreage
And planted it to vegetables to sell.
But then the war took off their hired men;
The fields grew up, to weeds and bushes first,
And then the fields were thick with ashy pine.
The faces of prosperity and luck
Turned westward with the railroads from New England.
Poverty settled, and the first went off,
Leaving their fathers' forty-acre farms,
To Manchester and Nashua and Lowell,

And traded the Lyceum for the block.
Now the white houses fell, among the wars,
From eighteen-sixty-five, for eighty years,
The Georgian firmness sagged, and the paint chipped,
And the white houses rotted to the ground.
Great growths of timber felled grew up again
On what had once been cultivated land,
On lawns and meadows, and from cellar holes.
Deep in the forest now, all out of place,
The reddened rails of an abandoned track
Heaved in the frosts and roots of the tall pines;
And there an antique locomotive stood,
Red as the fallen needles,
Heavy with vines, and perfectly immobile.

The farmer worked from four and milking time
To nine o'clock and shutting up the hens.
No kind of work availed; midwestern plains
Competed with one man on a rocky hill.
The heavy winter fattened him; the spring
Unlocked his arms and made his muscles lame.
By nineteen-forty, only the timid young
Remained to plow or sell; the others, strong,
Could earn a city wage. Divorced from earth,
From pain of birth, from sight of death removed,
They lived to be amused. For fifty years,
He was the noble man in the sick place,
Who saw the city's anarchy return
To set its nameless chaos in the woods.
All images of our magnificence,
The buildings inching taller, and the road
Down which the pioneer discovers West,
Become concentric in a heavy dark

Where four or five degraded pairs of eyes
Follow small actions on a tiny screen.
Who is to say my country is the end,
Or the beginning? except my friends and I.
Unless we can disprove predicted death,
The jungle or the sea will take New York,
And threat of plague; or maybe we will sink
All to the idiocy of daily bread.
I number out the virtues that are dead,
Remembering his soft consistent voice
That sharpened on the difficult to tell,
His honesty, his subtlety, and most,
The bone that showed in each deliberate word.
Another rank of virtues was his trade's,
His working love of animals and land—
No rhapsodies, but hands that shaped and made
Domestication of the wilderness;
For with his honest tongue and subtle eyes
And knowledge of the malice of the earth,
He was the agency of civilization.
Beasts of disorder wait in every place,
Inhabiting the dark,
Ready to leap if one more light goes out.

The length of Wesley Wells, those miles away,
Today was carried to the lettered plain
In Andover, nearby the store he worked,
While March bent down the cemetery trees.
I stand alone on England's crowded shore
Where storm has driven everyone inside.
Though here I have such friends as few men have
Who work a lifetime at it, though I know
Nostalgia for the quiet of this place,

My place and people are for sure across
The hooded wind and barbarous Atlantic
In dark New Hampshire where his widow wakes.
I think across to him, old man I loved,
The tall and straight, bent in a clumsy box.
I mourn the dead old man, of a sick place.
I number out the virtues that are dead.
Soon I will come to cross the hilly sea,
And take my work again,
And walk again, among the familiar hills.

7. Marriages

WEDDING SPEECHES

GROOM:

The welter world unhinges me: I send
A whirling way my crying toward your face,
But you are distant, and you do not tend
My agonies with your unmeasured grace.
O let us touch and mend
The mazeful tatters of this wedding lace.

BRIDE:

White in the crowd is perfect, and the white
Against the blur of backgrounds is a word
Of pure contentment, and a moveless light
For you who flit as crazy as a bird.
O sink upon my bright
And certain breast, where misery is blurred.

GROOM:

Now I have told your name, my certain girl,
Against the fruitless winds, and I am found,
Secure against the rumor and the swirl,
And fastened like a pillar to the ground.
O let us waltz and whirl
Through ballrooms filled with festivals of sound.

BRIDE:

I am too naked for this dance. I fall
Away from you, your solid arms and face.
I cringe against the white and fainting wall.
My gown is tatters, and not wedding lace.
O let us kneel and call
God Hymenaeus to this sacred place.

EPITHALAMION
FOR KIRBY THOMPSON HALL
SEPTEMBER 13, 1952

Now she comes moving on the whirling aisle.
I praise her beauty now
Who tall and pale comes moving on the aisle,
Erect, whose hands allow
No motion but of love and dignity,
And stay the shuddering sea;
Whose stateliness
Protects a wilderness
Of joy.
And I,
Witnessing by this marriage Kirby made
Most beautiful,
Grow in my strength as storm- and sea-winds fade,
For on the bed of love the heroes play
Who are the poem of our wedding day.

Yet we are parted by our humanness,
Not touching hand to hand.
We do not stand
In full reflection of another face
But haunt in singularity
An unfamiliar place,
Lost from all station in reality.
And now within the whirling church
Comes chaos swinging from the dark;
We cannot halt such vertigo to search
A solid mark.
No. It is by choice and form
We build defenses from the storm,

Imposed upon vacuities of space.
And so we summon heroes who must say
They are the poem of our wedding day.

Out of the whirling images and sound,
They march to take our names,
Whose formal feet attend the formal ground,
Who play our games.
We all must choose
Moments of light to flash against the screen,
And build, not lose,
The planned and formal characters we mean.
By form and fashion, we
Have come from the incomprehensible sea
To this hard shore.
Though irony marks the mind's unwilling core,
We in our formal character
Will live together.
So let our heroes laugh, and let them play,
And waltz together on our wedding day.

EPIGENETHLION: FIRST CHILD

My son, my executioner,
  I take you in my arms,
Quiet and small and just astir,
  And whom my body warms.

Sweet death, small son, our instrument
  Of immortality,
Your cries and hungers document
  Our bodily decay.

We twenty-five and twenty-two,
  Who seemed to live forever,
Observe enduring life in you
  And start to die together.

I take into my arms the death
  Maturity exacts,
And name with my imperfect breath
  The mortal paradox.

MARRIAGE: TO K.

When in the bedded dark of night
I touch your body huddled tight,

Though each is singular and free
In numerous humanity,

I have some special knowledge then
That crosses and will cross again.

1

I took a sea shell home when I was nine
    And stuck it in a box
In an attic storeroom which was wholly mine,
    Where I kept rusted guns, and rocks
        Incarnadine.

The sea shell often pleased me most, because
    It took me far away,
To green reptilian seas, the space there was
    Before the nervous human day
        Shattered the pause.

Held to my ear, it reminisced for me
    Of bird and fish and ocean,
Of storms recorded, roaring distantly
    With swoop of winds and crashing motion
        From a brute sea.

Where do illusions come from? When I was four
    I thought a hill nearby
A giant sleeping, whose long body bore
    A layer of earth. His waking cry
        Would mean a war.

I thought school would be purple. It was brown,
    And usual to see.
The teacher sat upon no jeweled throne.
    I had foreseen a luxury
        Far from my own.

Collecting things became the only fun
    To please me while I grew.
Sea shell or colored rock or rusted gun
    Replaced illusions lost with new
        Possessions won.

Each errand on the private attic stair
    I fled in misery
From change for which no warning could prepare.
    These losses which were good for me,
        I had to bear.

The daily loss created by the child,
    Who wants to keep on growing,
Makes new activity appear defiled;
    Men win at last to some self-knowing
        Unreconciled.

The body situates the reeling soul
    By annual increment
Until the body, not the mind, is whole;
    The years upon the stair were spent
        Without control.

2

Today, the father of a ten months' boy,
    Who cries to grow the faster,
I climbed the attic staircase to enjoy
    The place again where I was master
        Of every toy.

109

I held the sea shell to my ear and heard
    The blood that pounded in it,
Blood of myself, and blood of him inferred
    Who found a distant sea within it;
        Of the sea, no word.

To be deprived of pterodactyl seas
    And of the easy lie—
No one can say there is a loss in these
    But of romance, to multiply
        Fictions that please.

The sea that flooded at my head was new.
    The introspective shell
Reported what the times declared was true:
    "Each man is home within the hell
        His thoughts construe."

Only the single man, wholly alone,
    And in a childish room,
Holding the objects that were once his own,
    Spelled out the singular small doom
        Of flesh and bone;

Finally growth was nowhere; now was then;
    I heard the pulse-beats ply
And drifted on a manless sea again,
    Anonymous, alone, and I
        Was like all men.

I took the shell away. It was not true.
    The noises of the street
That I had closed an ear on, now came through
   The attic window to repeat
      What men must do.

I was deprived of easy loneliness,
    The latest luxury;
I put the shell away in its recess.
   It told no real, imagined sea,
      But lied no less.

I took the stair again, and said good-by
    To childhood and return,
Nostalgia for illusion, and the lie
   Of isolation. May I earn
      An honest eye.

Index of Titles and First Lines

Index of Titles and First Lines